Squacky Is
Afraid of the Dark

RP | KIDS

PHILADELPHIA · LONDON

Printed in China

Books published by Running Press are available at special discounts for bulk purchases in the United States
by corporations, institutions, and other organizations. For more information, please contact the Special Markets
Department at the Perseus Books Group, 2300 Chestnut Street, Suite 200, Philadelphia, PA 19103,
or call (800) 810-4145, ext. 5000, or e-mail special.markets@perseusbooks.com.

ISBN 978-0-7624-5021-3

Library of Congress Control Number: 2013939235

9 8 7 6 5 4 3 2 1
Digit on the right indicates the number of this printing

Art adapted by Joe Mathieu
Designed by Frances J Soo Ping Chow
Text adapted by Ellie O'Ryan
Edited by Marlo Scrimizzi
Typography: Vag Rounded and Univers

Published by Running Press Kids
An Imprint of Running Press Book Publishers
A Member of the Perseus Books Group
2300 Chestnut Street
Philadelphia, PA 19103–4371

Visit us on the web!
www.runningpress.com/kids

The sun was starting to set. It would soon be time for bed. But there was still time for one more game: hide-and-seek.

"Where are the other Pajanimals?" Apollo asked.

Then Apollo heard a giggle coming from the curtain. He peeked behind it—and found Cowbella.

"Now you can help me find the others," Apollo told her.

Apollo and Cowbella were so busy looking for Squacky and Sweet Pea Sue that they didn't notice when someone snuck up behind them. It was Sweet Pea Sue! Everyone started to laugh.

"Found you!" Apollo exclaimed.

"Now let's go find Squacky," Apollo said.

"But we've looked everywhere," replied Cowbella.

Apollo noticed that the closet door was open a crack. "But not in the closet," he whispered.

Everybody hurried over to the closet. Sweet Pea Sue pushed open the door. "A-ha!" she said.

"Ahhhhhhhhhhhhhhhh!" Squacky yelled. He ran out of the closet as fast as he could.

"What's wrong, Squacky?" asked Sweet Pea Sue.

"Well . . . QUACK . . . I was hiding in the closet, then I realized . . . QUACK . . . it was dark," Squacky tried to explain. "And then I realized it was really dark . . . QUACK-QUACK . . . and then I realized it was too dark. . . ."

"Okay, it was dark. But what's wrong with that?" Apollo said.

"Because when it's dark, I don't know what's in the closet with me!" Squacky cried. "There could be a sea monster, or slimy worms, or canned beans!"

"Squacky, there's only clothes in your closet," Cowbella said.

But Squacky wasn't sure. "Really?" he asked.

"Yes. It's just your imagination," Sweet Pea Sue said.

"Well, my 'magernation' does not like the dark!" Squacky announced.
He gave his blankie an extra big hug.

"I know what will cheer you up," said Sweet Pea Sue.

"Oh yes," Apollo said. "A little bounce, right, Squacky?"

Then all the Pajanimals did a special dance—the Pajama-Rama-Bounce!

When they finished dancing, Squacky flopped down on his bed. "Now I'm sooo tired," he said.

"Five more minutes till bedtime, Pajanimals," Dad called from the hallway.

"We need to brush our teeth," Apollo said. Everyone followed him into the bathroom.

"Now where is that toothbrush?" asked Squacky. As he searched for it, a towel fell on his head. "Who turned the light out?" Squacky cried.

"You okay, Squacky?" asked Sweet Pea Sue.

"No, I am not! I do not like the dark. At all!" Squacky replied. He shook the towel off his head.

"We know, buddy. But come on—we've gotta get ready for bed," Apollo replied.

After they brushed their teeth, the Pajanimals curled up in their cozy beds.

"Good night, Pajanimals. Sleep tight. See you in the morning light,"
Mom said.

"Good night," the Pajanimals replied.

CLICK. Mom turned out the light.

Squacky sat up in his bed. "Why'd it get so dark?" he cried.

"Because Mom turned the light off . . . like she does every night," Apollo said.

"Yeah, but it's super dark," Squacky said. "I can't see the end of my bed! What if there's something there . . . like a pink platypus?"

"There's nothing there, Squacky, I promise," Sweet Pea Sue said.

"Get some sleep, Squacky. Good night," said Cowbella.

Squacky tried to fall asleep. But it was just too dark. "Um, guys?" he said in a scared voice. "It's super, duper, infinity dark! QUACK!"

"Squacky, do you need some help?" asked Sweet Pea Sue.

"Yes!" Squacky exclaimed.

"I know what we should do," Apollo said. "Come hop on my bed."

The other Pajanimals scrambled onto Apollo's bed.

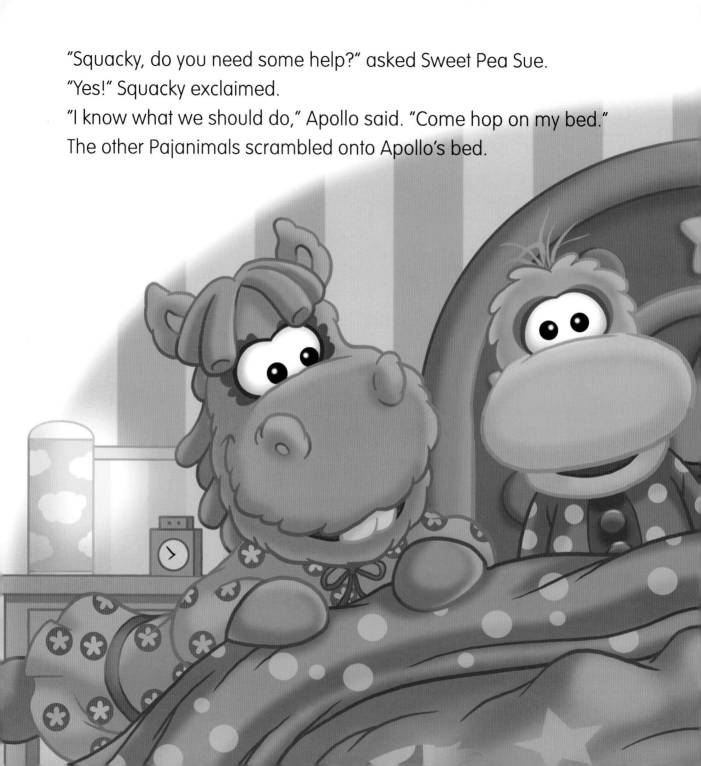

"Ready?" Apollo asked.

"Ready!" said the Pajanimals.

"Let's bundle up, snuggle up, huggle up, and go!"

Suddenly, Apollo's bed turned into a rocket ship! The Pajanimals floated outside in a cloud of golden sparkles. The night sky was beautiful, and even though it was dark, Squacky didn't feel scared at all.

"Oh, look," Sweet Pea Sue said. "There's the moon!"

"Hello, Pajanimals," the Moon said. "What brings you to my night sky tonight?"

"Well, Squacky couldn't sleep," Sweet Pea Sue explained. "He doesn't like the dark."

"Actually, my 'magernation' doesn't like the dark," Squacky corrected her.

"I understand," the Moon replied kindly. "It feels scary when you can't see that well in the dark, and you imagine things that aren't really there. But, you know, Squacky, that 'scary stuff' is not real. You are always safe and sound in your bed."

"Really?" Squacky asked.

"Yes. And remember, there is one light that is always on," the Moon continued.

"There is?" said Squacky.

"Why, yes—me!" the Moon said. "Even when you can't see me, I am shining down on you, watching over you while you sleep. Do you feel better, Squacky?"

"Sort of . . . well . . . yes! Squacksolutely!" Squacky said.

"Then it's time to go home, my friends," the Moon said. "Good night, Pajanimals. See you soon!"

Back at home, Apollo gave something special to Squacky. "I thought you might like my Rocket Light on your table tonight," he said. "It'll remind you that . . ."

"The Moon is up in the sky, always watching over me," Squacky said. "Night night!"

Then the Pajanimals fell fast asleep . . . and had sweet dreams all night long.